ɿefer Hirshberg (aka Nona) is a retired communications
ecialist with a master's degree in literature. Her career
cluded positions as an assistant professor of literature
d composition, a freelance writer for *The Washington
Post* and staff journalist for *The Washington Star*,
ernment positions in communications and public affairs,
d president of a communications and public relations
ompany. Throughout her career, she wrote news and
ature stories, proposals, speeches and op-eds. Since
etiring, she has turned her writing skills to children's
stories and poetry.

iends,
owers &
nces
VENTURES OF
AND SILAS
NONA HIRSHBER

Ordering Information
Quantity sales: Special discounts are available on qu
purchases by corporations, associations, and others. For d
contact the publisher at the address below.

Publisher's Cataloging-in-Publication data
Hirshberg, Nona
Friends, Flowers & Fences

ISBN 9781647503796 (Paperback)
ISBN 9781647509163 (Hardback)
ISBN 9781647509170 (epub e-book)

Library of Congress Control Number: 2021915085

www.austinmacauley.com/us

First Published 2021
Austin Macauley Publishers LLC
40 Wall Street, 33rd Floor, Suit 3302
New York, NY 10005
USA

mail-usa@austinmacauley.com
+1 (646) 5125767

'ends, *Flowers & Fences* is dedicated to my grandson,
as Greis, and my twin sister, Mimi Walkington, both of
whom inspired these stories.

ly thanks to my husband, Robert Weinberger, for his
fidence in me and his proofreading skills. Also, to Herta
Feely for her encouragement.

Chapter One
Jack Learns Something

Once upon a time, there was a little boy named Jack. Jack had red hair, blue eyes, and a big smile that made everybody happy when they saw him. Jack was five years old.

Jack's new house was on Cedar Road, which was a ve long dirt road that curved to the right at one end. You might think the road had cedar trees growing along the since it was called Cedar Road, but it didn't.

Jack was not allowed to walk by himself to where the road curved, but his mommy or daddy would sometime walk with him. He WAS allowed to go across the street c visit Farmer Jones who owned a truck farm.

At first, Jack thought that Farmer Jones planted and trucks on his farm and he imagined big red trucks poppi out of the ground and little yellow trucks pushing up the and green and blue trucks zooming up and down the rc of dirt. But that would be very strange, indeed!

Then when Jack moved into his new house and saw t farm, he realized a truck farm was a flower and vegetable farm.

And when Jack looked across the street from his bedr window, he saw purple pansies and red roses and yellow daffodils and all sorts of other flowers he didn't know th names of—yet.

And beyond the flowers there were red and green tomatoes, and orange and yellow peppers, and green cucumbers, and artichokes, and his special favorite—gre beans. (He especially liked the way his mommy cooked them with butter and salt and just a light shake of black pepper.)

Jack later learned when he was a very big boy that a truck farm is called a truck farm because the things it g are taken to market in the back of a truck!

Mr. Jones was a very nice man and a very good farm Sometimes he would show Jack how he planted seeds, a watered them, and made sure they got enough sun so t would grow.

He tended to his farm every day, including on the weekends. Mommy and Daddy exercised on the weeke but Farmer Jones worked.

One day Jack heard his big sister, Ruthie, talking to thei mother and asking what she would like for Mother's Da Jack remembered that once a year sometime around n was Mother's Day. It was a day to do special things for Mommy. Or to give her presents that would show ho much he appreciated all the things she did for him like:

- washing his clothes, and
- shopping for food, and
- cooking dinner, and
- taking him to swimming lessons, and
- especially, reading him stories before tucking him i bed at night.

Jack had been saving up any money he got so that h
could buy something nice for his mommy. He had $8.37.
Grandpa had given him $2.00 to spend at the zoo. And
daddy had given him $3.00 for helping him mow the la

$3.00 were from Aunt Sofia who had sent a check fo
Christmas from Minnesota where she lived.

And the other $.37 he got from Ruthie who only wan
paper money in her new wallet, and so she would give J
any loose change she had after buying her school lunch.

Jack got the idea that he would get his mommy a beau
flower for Mother's Day to show her how much he loved
And, of course, he thought that Farmer Jones would be j
the grownup to help him choose the very best one.

So one day a couple of weeks before Mother's Day, Ja
went to see Farmer Jones while his mother was out shop
He wanted this to be a big surprise for her, and so he we
when she wouldn't know what he was doing.

Jack explained to Farmer Jones that he wanted a pre
for his mommy for Mother's Day.

"Oh, what a good idea," said Farmer Jones. "Do you
to buy her a bouquet of flowers? Or a plant? Or a trellis
plant she already has? Or an ornament for her garden?"

Now Jack was really confused. "I don't know, Farmer
Jones," he said. "Will you help me decide? I have $8.37
to spend."

"Well," said Farmer Jones, "that is a very sensible way
shop—by letting me know how much money you have t
spend. We could choose any one of the things I mention
but I have a special plant in mind that will last the whol
summer and then come back again the next spring—it i
called a gardenia, and it smells so good. And I have one
that costs exactly $8.37."

Jack wanted to see the gardenia right away. But wh
he looked at it, he was disappointed because he knew
that purple was his mommy's favorite color, and garder

white. They did smell wonderful—but no, he knew he
ed something purple.

o you have anything that is purple?" he asked. "That is
my's favorite color."
h," said Farmer Jones, "in that case, yes! They don't
the smell of a gardenia, but they will last and last,
f you plant them outside, they will revive in the spring.
hey come in all kinds of colors too, including purple——
es!"
ck looked at the pansies and realized that this was the
ame flower he saw when he looked out his window.
rimmed the farm—at least the part he could see—and
ew his mother loved pansies.
weet little faces," she would say. (And if you really
d carefully at a pansy, it seemed like there was a face
ng back at you.)
it was decided! Jack was very happy. He bought as
pansies as his $8.37 would buy, enough to put into one
ot making a beautiful plant.

ummed a little song to himself as he crossed the
ry road and went into his house. His mommy wasn't
yet, so he had just enough time to figure out a place
le the present before she arrived.
went up to his room.
at would be the best place, he thought. *But where?*
ny came into his room in the morning to wake him up
t night to read him a story and put him to bed. So he
n't just leave the plant on his bureau or bedside table
ise she would see it.
e also came into his room to get his dirty clothes from

the clothes basket and to hang them back up once they were clean. So there didn't seem to be any place he cou hide his present without his mommy seeing it!

Then Jack remembered that way in the back corner his closet, under the hanging clothes on the right side, w little dark place where he used to hide from his sister if t were playing hide-and-seek. He figured this would be a good place to hide the pansies until Mother's Day.

Jack was so pleased with himself. He kept thinking h surprised his mommy would be. He imagined the morni he would get up early and go downstairs with Ruthie to help make French toast for Mommy. (Daddy would be supervising.) They both would be surprised when he put pansy plant on her breakfast tray and started upstairs. Mommy would clasp her hands together with delight w she saw the tray.

A day before Mother's Day, Jack went deep into his closet to get the pansy plant. He thought he would put bow around it to make it extra special before giving it t Mommy. But when he brought it out into the light, he began to cry.

His beautiful pansy plant was all dried and shriveled looked like a dead bird he had once seen just off the pa the woods.

Jack didn't know what to do. Maybe he could buy

ıer plant? But he didn't have any more money. He
lered if Farmer Jones would have any ideas.
he rushed across the road with his plant, and wiping
tears he said to Farmer Jones, "Look what has
ened to my Mother's Day plant!" Jack was inconsolable
eyes filled up with tears again.

ırmer Jones was very kind. "Son," he said. "I think I can
is for you, but first let's figure out what happened.
lants are growing things. They need food and light
the sun and plenty of water—just like you and other
ing boys and girls. If you put a plant in the dark and
t from the sun and don't give it water, it will not stay
hy and will wilt and die."
ıt luckily, the plant still had some green leaves at its
and the farmer said that if they cut the plant back and
red it and gave it sunlight, it was sure to revive.
ıd that is what Jack and Farmer Jones did. They cut

back the pansy, pinched off its dead leaves and blossom watered it thoroughly and placed it on a sunny window the farmer's barn.

In the meantime, Farmer Jones gave Jack a replacemen pansy to give his mother the next day. And Jack agreed that as soon as his plant had come back to life, he woulc exchange it for the new plant Farmer Jones had lent hin

And the next day when Jack gave his mother the pur pansy, he told her the whole story and what he had lear about plants and how they need food and water and sun just like people, and how he would never make tha mistake again, and how good Farmer Jones was to him.

Jack's mother and father and sister were very proud the way Jack had worked things out.

That night when Jack went to bed, his mommy gave his usual cup of water as she tucked him in and kissed hi goodnight. Jack took a drink and thought for a minute then he reminded his mommy to check to make sure he pansy had plenty of water too.

Chapter Two
Jack Meets Silas and They Discover the Witches' Den

One spring morning, Jack woke up early and heard a ve
loud noise. It sounded like thunder, *grraboom!* but he co
see that the sun was out, and besides, thunder and light
storms don't usually happen in the mornings. His grandp
had told him that.

Jack scooted to the bottom of his bed and looked thr
the blinds out his window. He was amazed to see the bi
truck he had ever seen going right by his house and dov
the street. It was bright yellow with red letters on it. The
truck stopped two doors down from Jack's. *I wonder wh
that truck is doing here,* he thought.

He put on his clothes and went down to see if his mo
might know something about what a big truck was doi
the neighborhood.

"Hmm, oh," she said. "That must be our new neighbo
moving into the Johnsons' old house. Remember the Joh
moved last fall?"

ck was anxious to eat his breakfast as quickly as he
 so he could go down the street and meet the new
bors. His mother thought it was a fine idea.
e finished her coffee and toast while Jack ate his cereal.
 they put on their spring coats and walked out of the
. Ruthie decided to tag along with them. Jack was very
d. He hoped that the new family would have a little
or him to play with.

ey watched the moving men unload the truck and
boxes and furniture into the house, Jack looked around.
dn't see any people who looked like they were
ng in.

But soon, after about twenty minutes or so, a blue ca came to the house and parked behind the truck. Jack co see that a man was driving and a lady sat next to him i front seat. He also saw a head bobbing in the back seat.

When the doors opened and everyone got out, there was a little boy who acted a little shy at first. His eyes we looking at the ground and his hand kept touching the c door, as if he were afraid to let go. Or maybe it was so h could jump back in the car if he didn't like what he saw

Jack went up to the boy and said, "Hello, my name i Jack. What's yours?" The little boy looked up. He had bl eyes, and red hair, just like Jack. He looked a little taller than Jack and he wore glasses, which made him look ve handsome.

"My name is Silas," said the little boy. Then he gave J a big smile and said, "Let's play!"

MOVING
VAN

First Silas took Jack into his new house and showed h
all the rooms and, most importantly, the room where he
was going to sleep. They went upstairs to the third floor
and checked out the attic, and then went down into the
basement and looked at all the pipes and tried to figure
out which ones were for water, and which ones for gas,
which ones for the toilets. Very interesting.

And then they discovered a door that led to a very c
and dank place with several steps up to nowhere. It wa
pretty spooky, but they went up the steps anyway. Whe
they got to the top of the stairs, there were two big doo
that were kind of flat that opened to the outside by be
pushed up from the inside. You had to be pretty strong
open them, but Jack and Silas could do it together.

Once outside, they looked back and saw the place th
had come from. It didn't look quite so scary in the dayli
They lowered the doors back into position.

Then they rushed around to the front of the house to
all over again. They went back inside through the front
and down to the basement and to the door that opene
into the dark place.

"Wait," said Jack. "I think we could use a flashlight, sc
can see where the steps are and if there are any insects c
spidery things in the corners." Silas thought that was a g
idea because the space was very dark and while he like
insects and other living things, he didn't like to be surpris
by them.

"I know my dad has a big flashlight and a smaller or
Let's go ask him if we can use them."

"For what?" said his dad. "What do you need
flashlights for?"

"This is my new friend, Jack, and we are exploring an
found a secret place down in the basement that is very
So we need them."

"I think we packed them in that box over there on th
yard," as he pointed to one of the moving boxes. "But I
not sure. We have so many boxes!"

Silas and Jack soon found the flashlights and off they
went back down into the cellar. They had their flashligh
hand and turned them on, but the shadows the lights m
on the walls made things look spookier than before.

Silas was sure he saw a witch and a ghost in the shac
They came to the door with the steps behind it. "What c
you think this place is for?" asked Jack.

And why is it here? thought Silas at the same time.

"Looks to me like a perfect witches' den," screeched
voice in the dark that sounded a bit like a witch.

"Who is that!" shouted Silas as he jumped about a m
Jack quickly shone his flashlight toward where the voice
come from and saw that it was just his sister, Ruthie, try
to scare them. But then Jack thought, *This does look lik
den, and it is a perfect hiding place, and also would be
cool place to have a sleep over.*

"This could be our clubhouse," he told Silas.

ow about a witches' den?" said Silas. "Let's call this our Witches' Den . . . heh, heh, heh."
o you know much about witches?" asked Jack.
nd Silas said, "Well, I know the story about when there n "erumption" and hot lava was flowing down and a tornado came and ripped the house off the ground hen it landed on the Wicked Witch of the East and her. And the Wicked Witch of the West wanted the red slippers, but they magically went on Dorothy's feet. w the Wicked Witch of the West said, 'I'll get you, my , and your little dog Toto too! AHEEEHEH!'"
ck was visibly shaken and said, "And then what ened?"
Vell, stuff . . . and then Dorothy threw water on the to put out a fire and the witch started to melt! 'I am ng, melting,' she screamed. 'You cursed brat! Oh what a , what a world, what a wor . . .' and she was gone."
Ve could play that story again, right here in our Witches' Silas said. And so they decided that after Silas and his were all moved into their new house, Jack and Silas d fix up the Witches' Den.
ey swept it, and got rid of cobwebs and a spider or Silas's mommy gave them old pillows she was going to away. They brought candles down from upstairs. But my and Daddy said, "No candles, dangerous," so they o put them back.
ey planned to have a sleepover when the moon was in two weeks.

Chapter Three
The Haunted House

Soon it was Halloween and Silas and Jack asked their mommies if they could have a sleepover together in the Witches' Den at Silas's house.

It was a spooky night. The moon was covered by clou and it was very dark. They had trick-or-treated togethe right at dusk when the sun had gone down. They got lo of candy.

A couple of times they had gone up to a house and c scary pumpkin had greeted them, and at one house a g made of sheets had fluttered ominously in the wind. Oo that had sent shivers and chills down their backs.

But they were happy with all the treats they had go and they took their trick-or-treat bags to the Witches' D and laid out their candy on their sleeping bags. They ea had a flashlight and Silas's dad rigged up a lantern and hung it from a hook he fastened to a wall. So they had light by which to count their haul of candies (and eat sc of course).

Pretty soon Silas's mom let them know it was time tc out the lights and crawl into their sleeping bags for the They were wearing their clothes, so it really felt like they were camping out. They heard the wind pick up outsid something started howling.

Was it just the wind? Or did they hear some animal, ghost, or was it a monster? each of them thought.

Then Jack started to think of other things because he didn't want to dwell on the noise. Jack remembered tha had seen something earlier in the day and he wonderec Silas had seen it too?

"What?" asked Silas.

"Well," said Jack, "I saw a strange little girl walking b my house. I think she might live in that house up the str where the road turns to the right."

"What was strange about her?"

/ell, she was dressed in kind of blue rags and she had
dirty blondish brown braids and as she slowly ambled
, she was chewing on one of her braids. Yuck!"
as had seen her once before walking by his house and
as doing the same thing—sucking on one of her braids.
eard from his mom that her name was Karen, but he
want to go say "hi" to her because she looked too
.

both boys were going to sleep—they were so tired from
or-treating. *But,* thought Silas as he was falling asleep,
*if that howling noise is Karen and she is a prisoner in
ickety house up the street?* "Maybe it is a haunted
, and the haunts have captured the little girl with the
s," mumbled Silas to Jack.
ck thought about that for a moment and then he said
as, "Maybe you are right. Do you think we should go
re the situation? We could open these doors that lead
outside and slip out and I don't think anyone
d know."
as was excited by the plan, but then he thought about
my and Daddy and he didn't think they would like his
ing out of the Witches' Den. After all, Jack and Silas
supposed to be sleeping. BUT, it did sound tempting.
k was five-and-a-half years old, almost six really, and
vas just five and he didn't know if he was as brave as
Well, I guess there is just one way to find out, he said
nself. "Okay, let's," said Silas, and they put on their
and quietly pushed open the heavy double doors that
ed the Witches' Den to the outside, and slipped out in
ark. They were smart enough to bring their flashlights!

They slowly and quietly crept up the road toward the h
they now were sure was a haunted house!

Strangely, the closer they got up the road to the hou
the less loud was the howl they had heard in the Witche
Den.

They got to the front gate and then stopped. The ho
was dark, except for one light coming from an upstairs
window. The house looked broken down and pretty spo
The yard was just weeds instead of grass, and the walkv
was a broken path of concrete. Silas thought he saw
something cross over it.

Jack and Silas looked at one another. "Should we go
and look in the window?" Silas said to Jack.

"C'mon," said Jack as he tiptoed up to the front winc
Just then, there was a loud CRASH from inside. A windo
shade snapped up, and a shutter seemed to fall off its h
. . . And then . . . the door FLEW open. Jack and Silas we
frozen in fear, sure that a ghost or worse was about to g
them!

But instead, they heard a sweet voice from a little ol lady, who looked quite like someone's grandma. She hc a round rosy face, grey hair and wore a purple dress thc stretched to cover her plump body. "May I help you, bo Trick-or-treating is over. All our candy is gone!"

Silas and Jack were stunned. Of course they weren't t or-treating, they were out to explore what they though a haunted house.

The nice lady invited them in for a cup of cocoa since she had no more candy. The room was faded with old l furniture in old lady colors—pink and light blue and gre And right there on the coffee table were two cups of co as if she had expected them to come by all along! How strange!

She told Silas and Jack that they were very poor anc that was why the house was so broken down and the y mess. She just didn't have the money to keep things up. she was responsible for taking care of her dear little gre niece whose family had died in a car crash. The little gir name was Karen, and she was already asleep.

Jack and Silas felt really sad for Karen and for her n great aunt. They left the house to go back to the Witch Den and realized they had learned an important lesson about other people who might be less fortunate than they are.

When they got back to the Witches' Den, they again he that howling noise. And what do you know? It turned o be a neighbor's dog howling to be let indoors.

hen, Jack and Silas woke up. Their clothes were on and
hoes in the same place they had put them last night.
oors to the Witches' Den were closed—locked shut.
uld we have unlocked and locked those doors?
ered Silas. *Did we really go to the haunted house in the*
e of the night? Silas wondered if it was all a dream.
told Jack about the adventure and asked if he
nbered doing all those things.
d all Jack said was, "Wow, you do have exciting
ns, don't you!"

Chapter Four
Worms and TV

Jack and Silas were best friends now. They played just a
every day together, especially during the summer mont
when they could be outside.

They played hide-and-seek and marbles and jump
and baseball. They went exploring into the woods and
throughout the neighborhood. They pretended they we
knights in armor that were tasked by a princess to kill
on a mountaintop. Sometimes they were sailors fighting
monsters that threatened to capsize their boat in the se

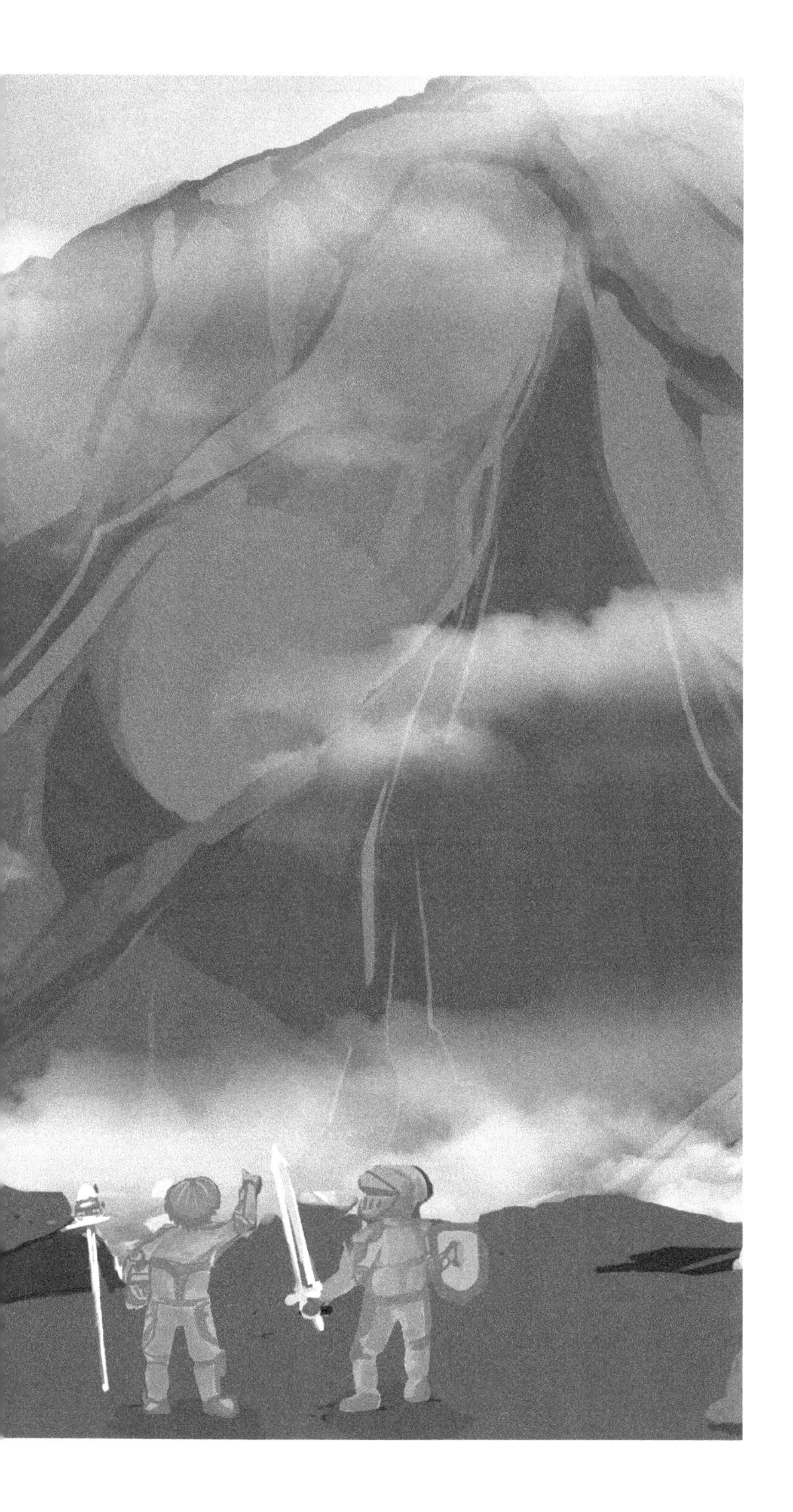

Jack's sister, Ruthie, played jacks, but Jack and Silas thought that was just for girls. Besides, it was hard to do because you had to do it one-handed. Throw the ball in air and collect the jacks. Before the ball bounced!

They never watched TV because then there wasn't a such thing as television. It is difficult to think of a time w there wasn't TV, but that was the case.

It hadn't been invented yet. Well, actually, it was bei developed, but so far no one in the neighborhood had t new invention.

One day they were hanging around when they saw Joh Fitzgerald. He was a little boy who lived a couple house down the street from Silas. He was six years old, and he wore pink nail polish on his fingernails, which Silas and J thought was strange. Nail polish was for girls, not boys.

Johnny liked to dig in his mother's garden. She had a big vegetable and flower garden on the side of her hou with a fence around it and a curved trellis archway thr which you entered the garden.

Jack wondered what kept Johnny so busy and intere in that garden. And then, that very day, they found out

Johnny was hunched over a pile of dirt and leaves in
back part of the garden when he suddenly pulled up hi
hand and shouted, "I've got one!"

"One what?" said Jack and Silas in unison.

"An earthworm." said Johnny. "I like to eat them in r
peanut butter and jelly sandwiches," and with that he r
to the back stoop and shouted for his mom who was in
kitchen making lunch.

"Oh yuck," said Silas and Jack.

"I don't believe that for a minute," said Jack who wa
older than Silas and probably knew.

But then Johnny's mother appeared at the kitchen d
and took the worm from Johnny and it seemed that sh
was, after all, going to put it in his peanut butter and je
sandwich.

Jack and Silas looked at each other and waited. Soo
backdoor opened and there was Johnny eating his sanc
He called to Jack and Silas and said, "Do you want a bi

No way, thought Silas.

And Jack said, "That is disgusting!" And then whispe
to Silas that he didn't really believe there was a worm i
the sandwich.

hen Johnny's mother returned to the door, she saw Jack
ilas and waved at them. Then she said something to
ıy that they couldn't hear. Johnny came over to them
aid, "Hey, guess what? We just got a television. Mom
ou can come in if you want to see it."
is was the first television in the neighborhood and Jack
ilas were amazed and very interested.
eally? Oh WOW" said both Jack and Silas at the same
"Yes."
ıt then Johnny threw a monkey wrench into the whole
"If you will eat a peanut butter and jelly sandwich
a worm in it, I'll let you come in and watch *The Howdy
y Show.*"
:k and Silas were torn. On one hand, they very much
ed to see this newfangled device called a television.
hey wanted to see what or who Howdy Doody was.
n the other hand, there was nothing they wanted
nough to make them eat a PB&J sandwich with an
worm in it.
et's see if we can trade with Johnny for something
d of eating the sandwich," said Jack.
kay, like what?" asked Silas.
'ell how about one of our trucks?"
truck?" complained Silas. "I'm not giving him one of
ucks! No, no, no!"

"But it's a trade negotiation," said Jack. "Maybe he w
take a truck instead of making us eat a sandwich with a
worm in it, and then we can watch TV. You do want to
and see the TV, right?"

"Right, but I don't want to give him one of my trucks
Oh, okay, but an old one."

Jack went back to Johnny and convinced him to take
red truck as payment for him letting them see television
instead of eating a worm.

And Jack and Silas were shown inside Johnny's house
into the living room and there was this little dark brown
But when you turned it on, it lit up and pictures appear
miraculous!—and then Johnny's mother turned the dial
voila! Howdy Doody and Buffalo Bob and all the kids in
Peanut Gallery and Clarabelle, the clown, were all there
pictures on the TV! It seemed like magic!

It would be a year before Jack and Silas's parents go
for their houses. In the meantime, every once in a while,
would be invited over to Johnny's house by Johnny's mo
and they would get to see TV. Not enough, mind you, b
was something.

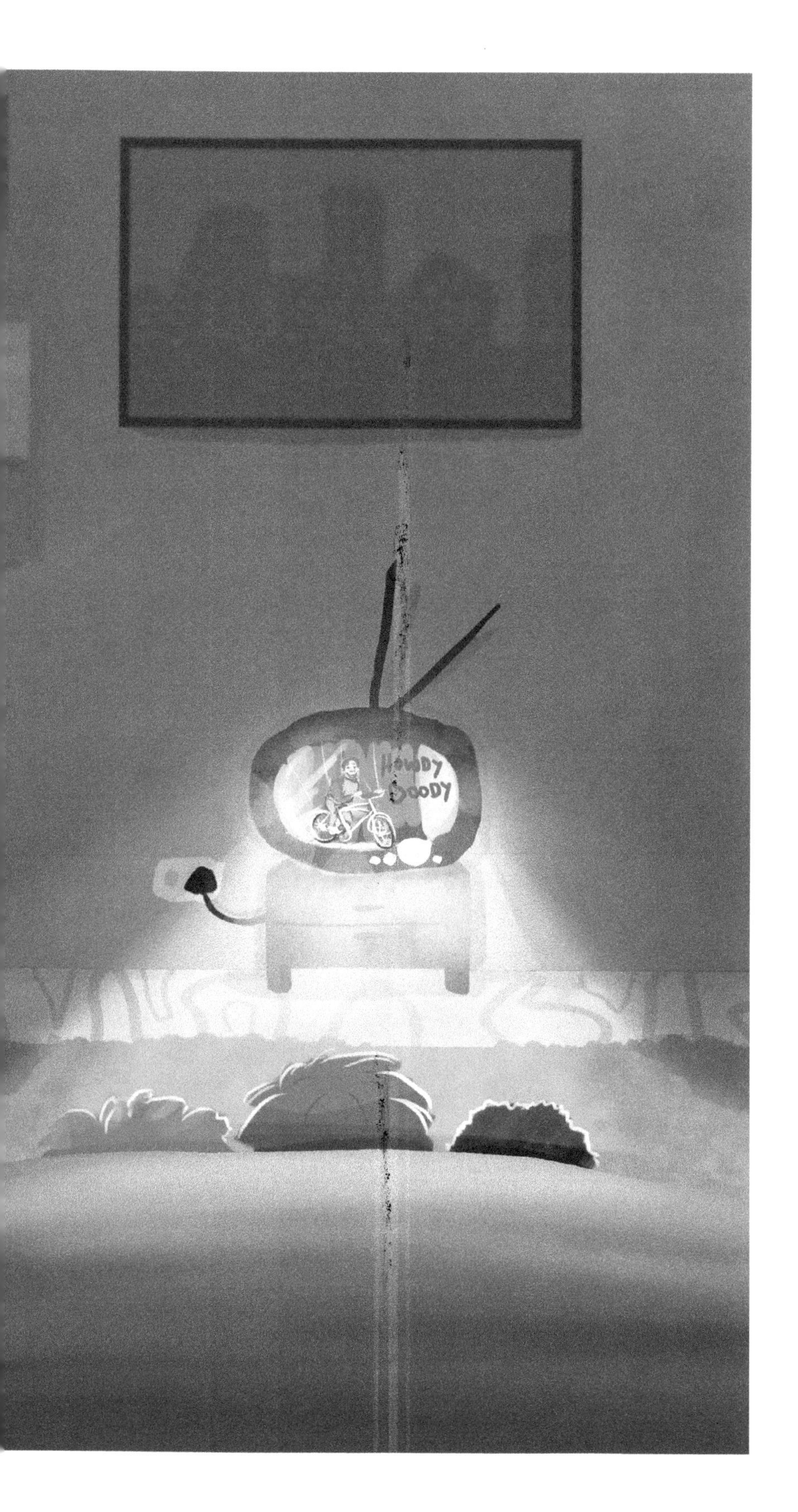
HOWDY
DOODY

Chapter Five
A Bully and Broken Arm

It so happened that there was one big problem in the neighborhood. That problem was named Georgie Little Georgie lived next door to Jack. He was the neighborho bully. He was always threatening someone—usually Jac and his sister Ruthie—that he was going to beat them u and do all sorts of mean things to them.

Unfortunately, anytime Jack and Ruthie, or Jack anc Silas, or all three of them together wanted to go down road to where Cedar crossed The Post Road, they had t right by Georgie's house. Fortunately, there was a fence front of his house, so sometimes they could pass by with him seeing them.

BUT, if Georgie was outside and could catch a glimp of them or if he heard them passing by, he would throw rocks at the fence and make loud scary noises, and call names, and tell them he was going to beat them up, ar generally, very unpleasant.

The truth is he was very unpredictable, and he was b for his age which made him even scarier.

Ruthie would tell Jack and Silas not to be frightened because, "Georgie is all bark and no bite," she would sa Ruthie was older, so she was a little braver than the other two.

One day Jack and Silas and Ruthie made a plan to The Post Road to watch a parade that was set to marc Cedar Road on its way to the Town Center.

As they started past Georgie's house, they heard a lo shout above their heads, and when they looked up, the was Georgie on a tree branch that was high enough to over the fence. He was right between the crook of the t and the branch over the fence, so he had a good perch could see them well. He also had a good escape route!

He told them they had better not pass by his house was going to come down and do something terrible to

"Oh yeah?" said Jack. "Like what?"

"Like you'll see, if you dare to do it," said Georgie.

"Oh, c'mon," said Silas to Jack and Ruthie. "Let's go." was feeling particularly brave that day. "What could he possibly do to us?" And he started to continue past Geor yard and was getting close to the tree where Georgie w hanging above the fence. Jack and Ruthie were close be when suddenly Georgie started to move along the bran

"OK, you asked for it," shouted Georgie. He had a m gleam in his eye and a terrible smile on his face. "I have axe in my garage and I am going to go get it, and I am going to chop your heads off. Just watch what I do," anc started to scramble down the tree.

At this point Ruthie, who was usually very brave, sai "Quick, let's get away from here!"

But Jack, who suddenly felt empowered by Ruthie's earlier bravery, stood his ground and said, "Don't worry Ruthie, he doesn't really mean it. Don't be afraid."

Ruthie, however, felt the danger, and knew that wh was happening was a lot more serious than the other threats Georgie usually made. And, besides, he had alre scrambled down from the tree and was on his way to the garage!

ck, Jack, he means it this time, really. We need to
way."
t Jack still stood firm and wouldn't move. So in
ration, Ruthie took ahold of Jack's arm and tried to
him away from the fence.
thie jerked his arm so hard that he was pulled off
ce, did a little air jump and fell on the ground, and
tarted to scream:
y arm, my arm. It hurts!" he cried, while tears started
am down his face. Ruthie noticed that Jack's arm was
ng in a way she'd never see an arm bend before!
vas broken!
k and Ruthie's parents were out that day, so they
n't go get help from them. Their great aunt Millie, who
ery old, was taking care of them, and she didn't know
o drive a car. So Silas ran quickly to his house and
oned his mother.

"Mom, Mom, come quick, there has been an acciden shouted Silas. "It's JACK! Help, help!"

When Silas's mother came out and saw what had happened, she knew right away that she needed to get to the emergency room at the hospital as soon as she cc

She got her car, and told Silas and Ruthie to get in t back, and Aunt Millie, who had come outside as soon a she had heard the commotion, held Jack on her lap in t front seat as they sped to the hospital. Jack was hollerin whole way, his arm hurt so much.

When they got to the hospital, Silas's mother parkec car in the parking lot and told Silas and Ruthie to stay while they took Jack into the hospital.

"Do not get out of this car while we are gone."

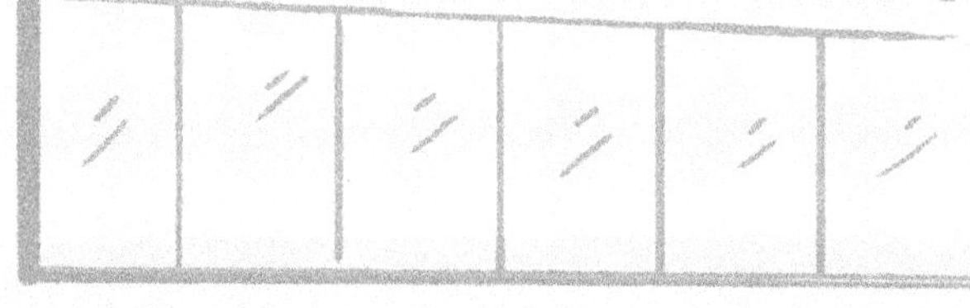
HOSPITA

Jack was in there a very long time. First Silas and Ru
just talked about what had happened and how mad th
were at Georgie Littlefield for being so mean. And Ruth
said she was feeling extra bad because it was her fault c
maybe she was going to get in trouble with her parents-
even though she was just trying to save Jack from Georg
axe.

Then they began to wonder what was going on and
it was taking so long for Jack to come out of the hospita

Soon they became very bored and wondered what
they could do. Silas's mom had said to stay in the car, b
she didn't say anything about rolling down the window
opening the car door.

They did both.

Silas noticed that there were lots of pebbles in the
parking lot, and he told Ruthie that he wondered how
pebbles it would take to fill up the car. The only way to
out, they decided, was to start scooping them up with t
hands and dumping them into the car. So they began!

Hours later (it seemed like) out came Silas's mom, A
Millie and Jack from the emergency room. Jack's left arr
was wrapped in a big white cast, and though he seeme
proud of his cast, he still had a pretty glum look on his f
He was remembering all the pain he had suffered.

When Silas's mom and Aunt Millie saw all the pebble
the car, they were horrified! "What have you two done?
asked Aunt Millie of Silas and Ruthie as she tried to get
the car.

And everybody, with the exception of Jack, had to st
putting the pebbles back onto the parking lot.

Silas's mom and Aunt Millie were not happy about t
but they were so relieved that Jack was all right and ha
been fixed up in the hospital, that they forgave Silas an
Ruthie and neither of them got punished.

tead, they all went from the hospital to the local
oppe and got big ice cream sundaes with all the
latey, gooey toppings.
ey all ate so much and so fast, Silas and Ruthie started
stomach aches on the way back home. Ruthie
ht that maybe this was her punishment, after all!

dtime, Silas was thinking over what happened that
ith Jack breaking his arm and the trip to the hospital.
hen he thought about other adventures he and Jack
nd the lessons they learned: about being a good friend,
eing kind to others who were less fortunate, and how
otiate for something you want, and how bullies can
bad things to happen.
remembered how Georgie hung over that fence on a
ranch.
n he wondered whether fences were good for keeping
in or keeping things out? The fence in front of
ie's house kept Georgie from getting them with his
3ut then a fence could also keep things out like rabid
nd other dangerous animals. And fences around
ns kept people from walking on flowers, and animals
ating the vegetables. But a fence between friends was
good. So were fences a good thing or a bad thing?
cided he'd talk that over with Jack tomorrow.
l as Silas fell asleep, thoughts about friends, flowers,
nces floated gently through his head.

GLOSSARY

Trellis	a structure of wood or metal used for supporting climbing plants. *Farmer Jones asks Jack if he might want to buy a "trellis" for his mother as a gift for Mother's Day.*	p
Supervising	watching over someone or directing how to do something. *Jack imagines his father "supervising" his and Ruthie's making French toast for their mother on Mother's Day.*	p
Wilt	to droop; for a plant to droop or become limp from not having enough water. *Jack saw his first plant "wilt" because it didn't get enough water or sun light.*	p
Revive	come back to life; get better. *Farmer Jones told Jack that his dead-looking plant would "revive" if it had water and sunshine.*	p
Replacement	something that takes the place of something else. *Jack got a "replacement" pansy for his wilted pansy.*	p
Dank	damp, dark, moist. *Silas and Jack found a "dank" place beyond a door in Silas's basement. It became their Witches' Den.*	p

e	to have turned a light (as from a flashlight) onto something in the dark. *Jack "shone" his flashlight towards the place where the voice in the dark came from.*	pg. 22
tion	outpouring or explosion of hot lava from a volcano. *Silas mispronounces the word "eruption". He says "erumption". Sometimes that happens when you are little and are learning new words.*	pg. 23
ously	in a scary or threatening way. *A Halloween ghost made of sheets fluttered "ominously" in the wind.*	pg. 24
l (on)	to focus on or think about something for a long time. *While Silas and Jack were in the Witches' Den on Halloween they heard a howling noise. It was scary and Jack didn't want to "dwell" on it.*	pg. 24
led	walked slowly. *Karen, the little girl who lived in the haunted house up the road from Jack and Silas, "ambled" along the road chewing on one of her braids.*	pg. 25
ts	ghosts and monsters who haunt houses. *As Silas fell asleep, he worried that Karen had been captured by the "haunts."*	pg. 25
ey ch	a snag or disruption in a plan. *Johnny Fitzgerald threw a "monkey wrench" into Silas's and Jack's plan to watch television by insisting they eat a PB&J sandwich with a worm in it.*	pg. 37

Newfangled	modern, present-day, the latest. *Jack and Silas very much wanted to see the "newfangled" device called a television.*	p
Crook	a curved or hooked shape; the bend in an arm, leg, or finger. *Georgie sat between the "crook" in the tree and a branch that hung over a fence.*	p
Perch	a place to sit with a good view of surrounding sights. *Georgie had a good "perch" on the tree in front of his house.*	p
Gleam	a look in someone's eyes that shows a certain feeling. *Georgie had a mean "gleam" in his eye that told Ruthie he was about to do something bad.*	p
Summoned	called for someone to be there; called to an action. *When Jack broke his arm, Silas quickly ran to his house and "summoned" his mother to help.*	p
Glum	unhappy, sad, depressed. *After Jack left the hospital with a cast on his broken arm, he still had a pretty "glum" look on his face.*	p

CPSIA information can be obtained
at www.ICGtesting.com
Printed in the USA
BVHW022041040122
625448BV00018B/760